D0274721

First published in German as *Der Weg zur Krippe*
© 1999 bohem press, Zurich, Switzerland
English version © 1999 Floris Books, 15 Harrison Gardens, Edinburgh
British Library CIP Data available
ISBN 0-86315-305-4
Printed in Italy

The Way to the Stable

A Christmas Story by Max Bolliger
Illustrated by Arcadio Lobato

Floris Books

There was once a shepherd who lived
in the hills near Bethlehem.

Although big and strong, he was
lame and could only walk with
crutches. So he mostly sat and tended
the fire on the hillside. He had a surly
tongue and the other shepherds were
afraid of him.

One amazing night, a choir of
angels appeared to the shepherds,
bringing them good news of a child
that was born to save the world.
The lame shepherd merely turned
away.

When the others set out to find the child that the angels had spoken of, he stayed by the fire. He watched them go, seeing the light of their lamps disappearing, smaller and smaller in the dark.

What was the point? he thought. They were chasing after nothing — a fantasy, a dream.

Now everything was quiet. The sheep were still. The dog didn't stir. He was surrounded by the silence of the night.

He poked the fire. But his mind was far away. He forgot to put fresh logs on the blaze.

Suppose it wasn't a fantasy? Suppose it wasn't a dream? Suppose ...

He got up and, taking his crutches,
began to follow the tracks of the other
shepherds through the snow.

At the end of the tracks, he came to a stable. Dawn was breaking. The wind was blowing up and there was a strange smell of spices in the air.

The ground outside the stable was full of footprints. He had found the place.

But where was the child, the
Saviour of the World?

He gave a bitter laugh. No angels, no child! Gloating, he turned to go back.

Then he noticed the little hollow in the manger, saw the shape where a child had lain in the straw.

And then he didn't know what
happened. For a long time, he crouched
in front of the empty manger. What did
it matter there was no child to smile at
him, no angels to sing, no mother
tending her infant?

He found no words to say what was
happening. Astonished, he got up to go.

After walking a little way, he
realised he had left his crutches in the
stable. He had to go back.

But why? he suddenly asked
himself, looking down.

Hesitating, he continued, but soon his steps became more and more joyful. Then he heard the welcoming shouts of the other shepherds and he strode forward to join his happiness to theirs.